Otter B

KIND

WRITTEN BY

Pamela Kennedy & Anne Kennedy Brady

ILLUSTRATED BY

Aaron Zenz

Tyndale House Publishers
Carol Stream, Illinois

FOCUS ON THE FAMILY®

Otter B: Kind
© 2019 Pamela Kennedy and Anne Kennedy Brady. All rights reserved.
Illustrations © 2019 Focus on the Family

A Focus on the Family book published by Tyndale House Publishers,
Carol Stream, Illinois 60188

Focus on the Family and the accompanying logo and design are federally
registered trademarks of Focus on the Family, 8605 Explorer Drive,
Colorado Springs, CO 80920.

TYNDALE and Tyndale's quill logo are registered trademarks of Tyndale
House Ministries.

Cover design by Josh Lewis
Cover illustration by Aaron Zenz

Book Design by Josh Lewis
Text set in Source Sans and Prater Sans Pro.

For manufacturing information regarding this product, please call
1-855-277-9400.

For information about special discounts for bulk purchases, please contact
Tyndale House Publishers at csresponse@tyndale.com, or call
1-855-277-9400.

Library of Congress Cataloging-in-Publication Data can be found at
www.loc.gov.

ISBN 978-1-58997-986-4

Printed in China

27 26 25 24 23 22 21
8   7   6   5   4   3   2

Otter B jumped out of bed. He ran over to his window. The sky was bright blue and filled with puffy clouds. What a perfect day for playing outside! Maybe Mama could take him and Franklin to the creek to go sliding down the muddy bank.

Otter B dashed into the kitchen.
"Mama! Can Franklin come over?"

"Not today, Otter B," said Mama.
"I just got a phone call. Franklin is sick."

"What's wrong?" Otter B asked.

"Franklin has a bad cough and a sore throat,"
Mama explained.
"He will have to stay inside for a few days."

Otter B frowned. Franklin was his best friend, and playing outside was their favorite thing to do. Otter B looked through the window. The wind made the leaves in the big oak tree rustle and the dandelions sway. He thought about the cool creek water and the slip-slidey mud.

"I really wanted to play with Franklin today,"
Otter B said with a sigh.

"I know," said Mama.
"I'm sure Franklin is disappointed, too."

Otter B thought about how Franklin was feeling.
It was probably no fun to have a bad cough and a
sore throat. Suddenly, he had an idea!

Otter B found a cardboard box.

He took the box and ran outside. He searched the backyard until he found just what he was looking for.

Otter B closed the box and pulled some of his favorite stickers
out of his pocket to decorate it. Then he took the box indoors.

"Mama, can I have some paper and glue and scissors and crayons?"

"What are you up to?"
Mama asked.

"I'm making something special for Franklin,"
Otter B declared.

He folded the paper, then cut out some shapes and colored them.
He glued them onto the paper and then drew a picture.

On the inside of the card, Otter B wrote a special note to Franklin.

"Can we walk over to Franklin's house, Mama?
I want to take him the cheer-up present I made."

Mama nodded. "We can go after lunch."

Otter B and Mama prayed before they ate. Otter B added,
"—and please help Franklin feel better."
Then Otter B ate his fish sticks in big bites and slurped down his milk.

"Now Mama?" asked Otter B as he helped carry their
dishes to the sink.

Mama laughed. "Okay, let's go!"

Otter B skipped in circles all the way to
Franklin's house. He rang the doorbell and waited.
Franklin's mama answered.

"What a nice surprise to see you!"
she said, smiling.

Otter B gave her the box and card for Franklin.
**"Can you tell him I'm really sorry he's
sick and that I prayed for him and that I
hope he can come out and play soon and
. . . Well, I guess that's it for now!"**

On the way home, Mama held Otter B's hand.
"What was in your present?"

Otter B grinned up at Mama.
"There's a yellow dandelion and a pretty leaf, three round stones, an acorn, and a ladybug! I decided that if Franklin couldn't play outside, I would give him some outside to play with inside!"

Mama laughed. **"What a kind friend you are, Otter B!"**

She gathered him up in a big hug. **"You thought about what would make Franklin happy, and you spent your day making it for him. I'm sure he knows just how much you care about him!"**

Kindness doesn't cost a thing,
and thoughtfulness is free.
So when you have a chance, be kind.
It's how you Otter Be!

Be kind and tender to one another.
Ephesians 4:32